First published in Great Britain in 2021 by Andersen Press Ltd.,
20 Vauxhall Bridge Road, London, SW1V 2SA, UK
Vijverlaan 48, 3062 HL Rotterdam, Nederland
Copyright © David McKee, 2021.
The right of David McKee to be identified as the author and
illustrator of this work has been asserted by him in accordance
with the Copyright, Designs and Patents Act, 1988.
All rights reserved.
Colour separated in Switzerland by Photolitho AG, Zürich.
Printed and bound in China.
1 3 5 7 9 10 8 6 4 2
British Library Cataloguing in Publication Data available.
ISBN 978 1 83913 094 6

ELMER
and the
Bedtime Story

David McKee

Andersen Press

Elmer the patchwork elephant was about to start an
afternoon walk when two young elephants appeared,
followed by their mother.
"Hello, Elmer," said the mother. "Please will you
look after Stella and Mel? I have to visit my sister."

"I'll be back late," she continued. "You'll have
to put them to sleep. A story will do it, like
the one about the flying carpet." She left.
"A tiring walk will do it as well," chuckled
Elmer. "Like the one we're going on."

They'd been walking for a while when a voice called, "Hello, Elmer! Are you babysitting as well?" It was Lion.

"Hello, Lion," said Elmer. "Yes I'm getting them tired so they'll sleep easily."

"Tell them a story, that will do it," said Lion.
"The one about the magic biscuit," said the young lions.

Elmer smiled. "Magic biscuit," he said.
"I could make one vanish!"

The walk took them to the river.
"Are you babysitting as well, Elmer?"
called Crocodile.
"Hello, Crocodile," said Elmer. "Yes, I'm
getting them tired so that they'll sleep easily."

"Tell them a story," said Crocodile. "That will do it."
"Tell them about the monster who lost his shadow,"
said a young crocodile.

"Oh, poor monster," said Elmer and walked on.

"This is nice and tiring," thought Elmer as they climbed a hill. Stella and Mel raced ahead and back again.

"Babysitting, Elmer?" called Monkey.

"Yes, I'm getting them tired so they'll sleep easily," said Elmer

"Tell them a story, that will do it," said Monkey.
"The one about the echo," said a little monkey.
"ECHO, echo, echo, echo…" said Elmer with a smile.

Next it was Rabbit.
"Babysitting, Elmer?" he asked.
"Yes," said Elmer, "I've been getting them tired
so they'll sleep easily."

"Tell them a story," said Rabbit. "That will do it."

"The one about the invisible teddy bear!" called a young rabbit.

"We'll see," said Elmer. "They must be tired because I am. We're nearly home."

Later, at home, Elmer said, "It's time to sleep."
The youngsters settled and said, "Please, Elmer,
tell us a story."
Elmer yawned. Slowly he started, "Once upon a
time... there were two brave elephants...
        called Stella and Mel...
                one day..."

Elmer woke as the youngsters' mother arrived.
She smiled. "A good story always works," she said.

"So does a good walk," said Elmer. "I never got to
'And they lived happily ever after'!"